To Ethan and Sophia

Bernice

"Oh my gosh it's a bear!"

by Rob Adamowski

illustrated by Kellee Beaudry

OctiRam Publishing
P.O. Box 5859
Vancouver, WA 98668
www.octiram.com

Library of Congress Cataloging-in-Publication Data
Adamowski, Rob
Bernice / by Rob Adamowski – 1st American ed.
p. cm.
Summary: Bernice is a big brown dog who is mistaken for a bear wherever she goes and learns a thing or two about bears and how it feels to be different.
ISBN 978-0-9830423-1-0
1. Dogs – Fiction 2. Bears – Fiction 3. Newfoundlands – Fiction 4. Pets – Fiction
5. Animals – Fiction
2010914245

First edition, 2011
Edited by Rebecca Brown, Blue Water Indexing
Cover and interior design by Julie Melton, The Right Type Graphics
The illustrations in this book were created in acrylic by Kellee Beaudry.

Printed in China
by Artful Dragon Press a U.S. Company
10 9 8 7 6 5 4 3 2 1
First American Edition

OctiRam Publishing
P.O. Box 5859
Vancouver, WA 98668
www.octiram.com

OctiRam Publishing supports the First Amendment and celebrates the right to read.

Acknowledgements

To my family
for your love and unfaltering support.
Thank you!
– Rob

With special thanks to Bernice, Camden, Hovering,
John, Julie, Kellee, Ramy, Rebecca and Scott.

This is Bernice.

Bernice has a thick, brown coat of fur
and eyes of gold.
And as you will soon see,
her story just had to be told.

Bernice is very, very big
and has a big appetite to match.
She'll eat almost anything,
but especially likes berries fresh from the patch.

Bernice has giant paws
that make swimming a snap.

She scares every fish in the river though,
when she jumps in with a powerful slap.

You might cross her path when out on a walk.
And when you see her lumbering by,
you'll know why people talk.

They don't mean to crowd, smile and stare.
But they all say the same thing;
"Oh my gosh it's a bear!"

Now it's true Bernice doesn't understand
everything she hears.
But not much slips past
her big brown floppy ears.

"It's a bear," they say, each and every one.
It happens so much;
Bernice knows what they'll say,
before they've even begun.

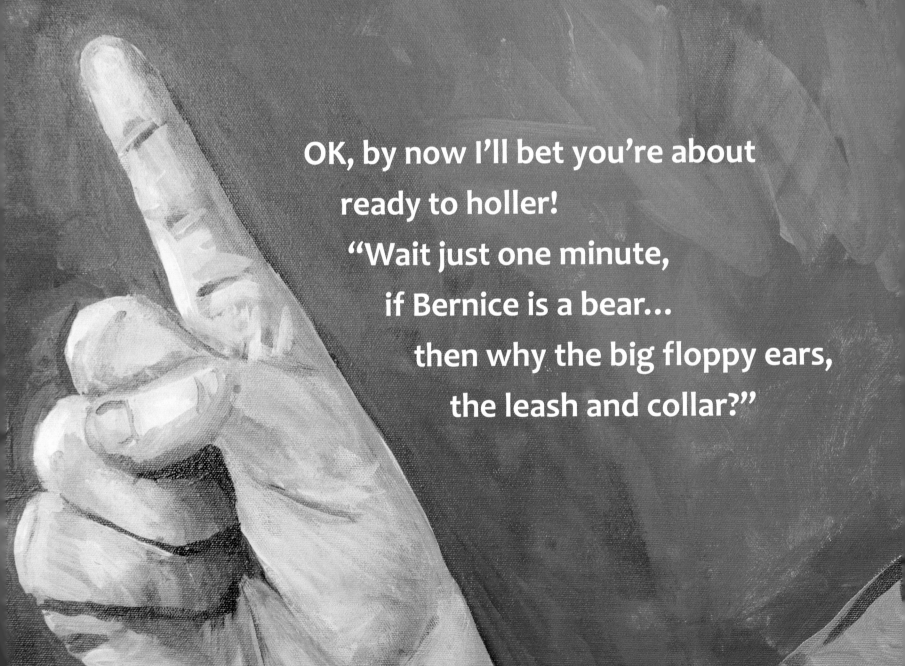

"It's a bear, it's a bear, it's a furry brown bear,"
she hears to her dismay.
Even when she's wearing a leash and collar,
which is just about every single day.

OK, by now I'll bet you're about
ready to holler!
"Wait just one minute,
if Bernice is a bear...
then why the big floppy ears,
the leash and collar?"

You're much too smart
to be fooled,
and as a matter of fact,

Bernice is actually a great big dog,
a Newfie or Newfoundland to be exact.

She doesn't like being called something she's not.
It makes Bernice sad and it happens a lot.

Up in the mountains.

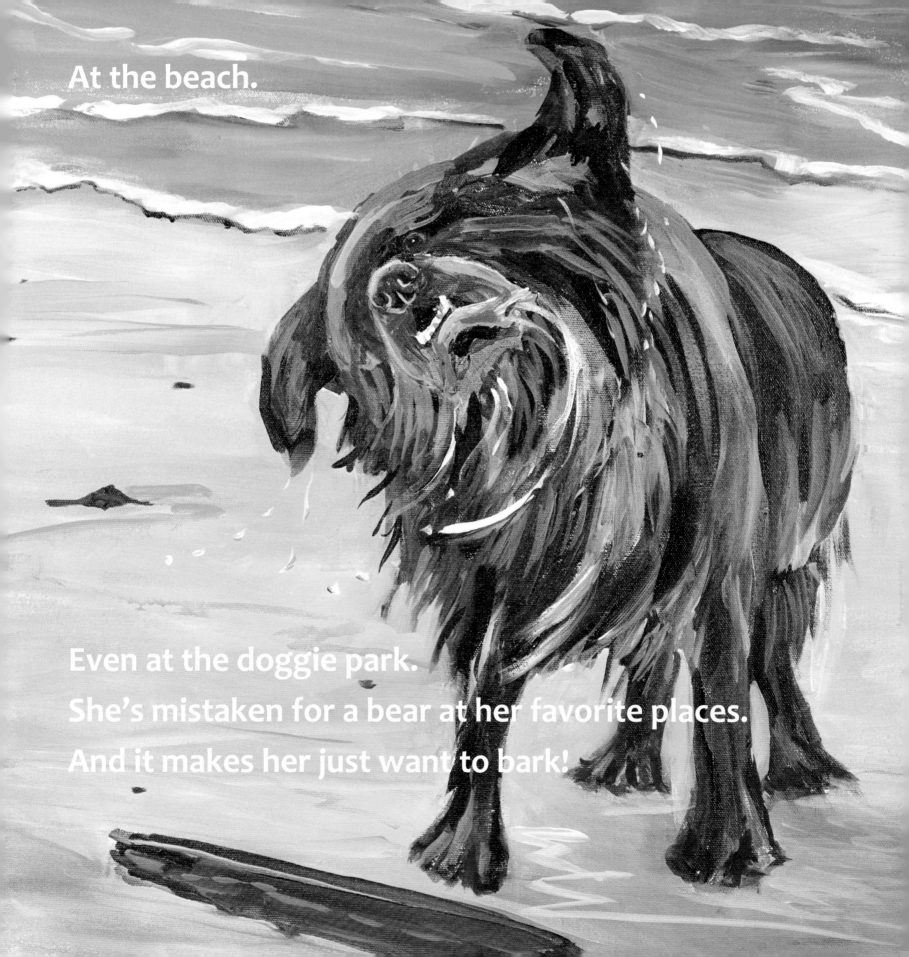

At the beach.

Even at the doggie park.
She's mistaken for a bear at her favorite places.
And it makes her just want to bark!

Bernice has never seen a bear,
but knows they can be very mean and scary.
The only similarity she sees,
is that she's big, brown and hairy.

However, Bernice is determined,
and as sure as bees buzz;
She would learn more about bears
and what's under their fuzz.

She asks her people parents
and they quickly reply;
"Bears are quite fantastic,"
but Bernice wants to know why...

They explain that "bears are often misunderstood." Her parents see them at the zoo,

the circus,

and even deep in the woods.

Bears can run, climb, swim and fish
and are really very smart…

In the winter while sleeping beneath the snow,
they say bears can even slow down their heart.

Suddenly Bernice feels proud
to have such distinguishing features.

Bears are really pretty amazing creatures...

Looking different than other dogs
is OK with her now.
Bernice knows she is different
and understands how.

As it turns out, people are totally fascinated with bears!
Now Bernice feels more like a famous movie star
when everyone crowds, smiles and stares!

"Oh my gosh it's a bear!"